A NOTE TO PARENTS

When your children are ready to "step into reading," giving them the right books—and lots of them—is as crucial as giving them the right food to eat. **Step into Reading Books** present exciting stories and information reinforced with lively, colorful illustrations that make learning to read fun, satisfying, and worthwhile. They are priced so that acquiring an entire library of them is affordable. And they are beginning readers with an important difference—they're written on four levels.

Step 1 Books, with their very large type and extremely simple vocabulary, have been created for the very youngest readers. **Step 2 Books** are both longer and slightly more difficult. **Step 3 Books,** written to mid-second-grade reading levels, are for the child who has acquired even greater reading skills. **Step 4 Books** offer exciting nonfiction for the increasingly proficient reader.

Children develop at different ages. **Step into Reading Books,** with their four levels of reading, are designed to help children become good—and interested—readers *faster*. The grade levels assigned to the four steps—preschool through grade 1 for Step 1, grades 1 through 3 for Step 2, grades 2 and 3 for Step 3, and grades 2 through 4 for Step 4—are intended only as guides. Some children move through all four steps very rapidly; others climb the steps over a period of several years. These books will help your child "step into reading" in style!

For three real doctors,
S.J.M., A.M.B., and W.C.Z.

 Published in the United States by Random House, Inc., New York, and simultaneously in Canada by Random House of Canada Limited, Toronto.

Library of Congress Cataloging in Publication Data: Ziefert, Harriet. So sick! (Step into Reading. A Step 1 book) SUMMARY: In three episodes, Lewis is sick, plays doctor with his friend Angel, and sees him get sick from eating too many cookies. 1. Children's stories, American. [1. Sick–Fiction] I. Nicklaus, Carol. II. Title. III. Series: Step into reading. Step 1 book. PZ7.Z487So 1985 [E] 85-1957 ISBN: 0-394-87580-X (trade); 0-394-97580-4 (lib. bdg.)

Manufactured in the United States of America 11 12 13 14 15 16 17 18 19 20

Step into Reading

So Sick!

by Harriet Ziefert and Carol Nicklaus

A Step 1 Book

Random House New York

Chapter 1: So Sick

"I feel sick,"
Lewis said.

"So sick!"

"Take this medicine,"
Mama said.

"Ugh!" Lewis said.
"I still feel sick."

"Have some pudding,"
Mama said.
"I'm not so hungry,"
Lewis said.

"Try some for me,"
Mama said. "It's good!"

"I'm still sick,"
Lewis said.

"Take a nap," Mama said.
"You will feel better."

Lewis took a long nap.

Lewis woke up.
He felt better.

"I'm not sick!"
Lewis yelled.
"I'm hungry!

"I want more
yummy pudding!
Then I want to play."

Chapter 2: All Better

Lewis said
to his friend Angel,
"We can play doctor.

"I will be the doctor.
You be sick."

Lewis put his ear
to Angel's chest.
He listened.
Thump! Thump!

Lewis said, "Cough.
Now cough again.
Again.
And again."

"Open your mouth.
Say AHHHHHH!
Say AHHHHHH again.

"All done,"
said Lewis the doctor.
"You are not sick."

"I know I am not sick,"
Angel said.
"But I'm hungry!"

Lewis said,
"We can get a snack."

Chapter 3: Snacktime

Lewis and Angel went to the kitchen.

Lewis took one cookie.
Angel took two cookies.

"I want more,"
Angel said.
"Not too many!"
Lewis said.

Angel took
three more cookies.
"Too many!"
Lewis yelled.

"Want to play now?"
Lewis asked.
Angel did not answer.
"You look sick,"
Lewis said.

"I am sick," Angel said.
"So sick!"

"Too many cookies!
You need medicine.

"You need a nap,"
said Lewis the doctor.

"But no pudding for you!"